The Black Stallion Returns

The Black Stallion Returns

by Walter Farley

A Storybook Based on the Movie

SCHOLASTIC INC.
New York Toronto London Auckland Sydney Tokyo

For Corky Randall and all the horse people
who made the Black Stallion films possible

Covers, endpapers, and photographs on pages 6, 16, 27, 34, 35 (bottom), 38, 40, 41, 42, 43 (top), 45, 47, 49, 51, 58, and 60. Copyright © 1982 by Tim Farley. All rights reserved.

Photographs on pages 10, 11, 12, 13, 14, 15, 18, 19, 20, 22, 23, 24, 26, 28, 31, 32, 33, 35 (top), 36, 37, 39, 43 (bottom), 44, 46, 48, 52, 54, 55, 56, 57, and 58. Copyright © 1982 by United Artists Corporation. All rights reserved.

Unit Photographer: Franco Bellomo

ISBN 0-590-72227-1

Text copyright © 1983 by Walter Farley. Text based on *The Black Stallion Returns,* copyright 1945 by Walter Farley. Copyright renewed 1973 by Walter Farley. All rights reserved. This edition published by Scholastic Book Services, a division of Scholastic Inc., 730 Broadway, New York, NY 10003, by arrangement with Random House, Inc.

12 11 10 9 8 7 6 5 4 3 2 1   3 4 5 6 7/8

Commonwealth Edition   Printed in the U.S.A.   14

This book, especially designed for young children, is a brief retelling of a famous book entitled *The Black Stallion Returns*, originally published by Random House in 1945 and now made into a major film. When children are a little older, they will want to read the whole story, which is much longer and more detailed than this picture book version.

The Black Stallion Returns

The summer night hung black and heavy around the barn. Then suddenly the silence was broken. There was the slow, creaky opening of an iron gate and the hushed sound of running feet over grass. A man in a white turban moved quickly towards the barn, stopping only once to glance back at the darkened house nearby. Satisfied that all was quiet, he crept to the barn door. In the shadows his dark face burned with excitement and anticipation. Soon he would face that devil horse Shêtân again! Soon he would destroy the Black Stallion! He reached into his pocket, removed the hypodermic needle with its deadly contents, and opened the barn door.

The Black moved to the front of his stall with the speed and agility of the wildest and most savage of animals. His thin-skinned nostrils quivered as he smelt the familiar scent of one he knew and hated. Gone was the even temper and calm he had come to know with Alec Ramsay. At this moment the Black's desert blood was inflamed with the instinct to protect himself. He

turned his bright eyes on the intruder coming towards him. Then he hurled forth his screaming challenge, and its shrillness shattered the night air.

The man moved fast, knowing the stallion's whistle would bring someone to the barn. He opened the stall door but fell back as the giant horse rose above him, mouth open, teeth bared. Staggering, the man lunged at the Black, but the horse's foreleg caught him in the groin. He fell down, rolling on the floor in an attempt to avoid the thrashing hoofs. The large medallion he wore on a chain around his neck

caught in a floorboard. As he scrambled to his feet and ran out of the barn, the medallion was ripped from his neck and fell to the floor.

The shrill sound of the Black's scream woke Alec Ramsay from a restless sleep. The boy lay still for a moment. Was his imagination playing tricks on him? Ever since the race in which the Black had beaten Cyclone and Sun Raider, Alec had feared for his horse's safety. The Black was so famous now, and so valuable, that almost anything could happen to him. Hardly a day passed that strangers—newsmen and visitors—weren't at the barn, watching every move the Black made. It's my fault, thought Alec. I had to prove to everyone that the Black is truly the fastest horse in the world.

The Black's scream shattered the night air again, and this time Alec knew it was not his imagination. Something very real was threatening his horse! He swung out of bed and rushed to the window in time to see a ghostlike figure emerge from the barn and disappear into the darkness.

Who was it? What had happened?

Terrified for the Black's safety, Alec ran from his room, down the stairs, and out of the house. When he arrived at the barn, he found the Black out of his stall. His eyes were bright with anger, and his coat was wet and lathered from his struggle.

"Oh, Black," Alec said, throwing his arms around the stallion's neck. "What happened?" Alec's hand swept over the horse's body, feeling for any sign of injury. To his relief he found nothing. His horse was all right—except for the anger still burning in his eyes. What kind of person had aroused so much fury in the Black? It must have been

13

someone the stallion knew and hated. But who was it?

It was then that Alec saw the large medallion lying on the floor. He picked it up. In its centre was a bird carved out of ivory, whose long, powerful wings were outstretched in flight. Two tiny red stones had been used for its eyes.

It was the bird of Arabia—a falcon used by men of the desert for hunting. Alec had seen many of them the summer before, when he was in the Far East visiting his uncle. Whoever had been wearing the medallion must have come from that part of the world. Why would such a person want to harm the Black? What possible motive could he have had?

Alec sat outside late into the night, watching the barn and studying the medallion. Now he regretted even more that he'd raced the Black. Before the race few people had known about the horse's mysterious past or about the terrible shipwreck that had brought him into Alec's life. Thinking of that stormy night on the Red Sea, Alec once again remembered the cruel men who had brought the stallion aboard the ship. Had they stolen the Black? If so, from whom? Where had the stallion really come from? Alec knew the answers to his questions lay in the stallion's past, somewhere in the desert, far away.

A few days later the worst of Alec's fears were realized. A visitor arrived—not one who sought to harm the Black but one who wanted to claim him for his own!

Abu ben Ishak was a great desert chieftain who had come from far across the sea. He had all the necessary papers to prove that the Black had been stolen from him. But Alec didn't need to see the papers to know that the Black belonged to this man. For Abu ben Ishak walked up to the stallion, unafraid, and spoke softly to him in Arabic. Alec heard the name "Shêtân" repeated again and again, and each time the Black's ears pitched forward, listening.

"You have been good to him," Abu ben Ishak told Alec, "and for that I am very grateful. Now I must take him home while there is still time."

"Time?" Alec asked, trying to keep the tears from his eyes. "Time for what?"

"What he was bred for," the chieftain answered. "The great race of the desert."

Abu ben Ishak said no more, and Alec, knowing he had only a few minutes left to be with his

horse, went to the Black. Would life be worth living without him?

"Hey, Black . . ." The words formed in his mouth but he could not get them out. The stallion lowered his head, the black mane falling down over his eyes. Alec pushed it away and rubbed his forehead as he'd always done. Then, realizing that it was the last time he'd hold his horse, his arms fell around the long silken neck and he pressed his head hard against the stallion.

"I would like to repay you for all you've done," Alec heard

16

Abu ben Ishak offer. "You have been good to Shêtân. I will be in your debt always."

"I don't need anything from you," Alec said without lifting his head. "I've had everything . . . everything anyone could ever want."

During the days that followed, Alec tried to adjust to a life without the Black, but it was hard. He went to school but couldn't study. He had trouble eating. He couldn't sleep, knowing he'd only dream of the Black, and it would make his loss hurt even more. His mother offered to buy him another horse, but no horse could take the place of the Black. Their love was special. Perhaps if he kept thinking how special it was, something would happen to bring them back together again.

It seemed that Alec's firm belief that he would see his horse again brought a visitor to his home a few weeks later.

His name was C. V. Volence. He was a breeder of racehorses in Kentucky and the owner of Sun Raider, one of the horses the Black had beaten in the big race.

Volence had read the news story of Abu ben Ishak's recovery of the Black and how grateful the old sheikh was to Alec Ramsay. Now Volence wanted to find the desert chieftain's home in the hope of purchasing horses from him. He knew Alec would be of great help since the sheikh was in his debt. Would Alec go with him? He would pay him well.

Would he go? Here was a chance to see the Black again! Alec found it difficult to restrain his joy. But how could he convince his mother to let him make such a long trip?

"School's almost over for the summer, Mum," he told her, "and this trip will be really educational, maybe even more than being at school. Besides, Mr. Volence has lots of friends in Arabia, and they'll help us find Abu ben Ishak's kingdom. We won't have any trouble at all. Please, Mum."

"I'll talk to Mr. Volence about it, Alec," she answered, concern showing in her eyes. "I'll talk to him, but I'm not promising anything."

The next day Alec's mother went to see Mr. Volence. Later

that night, when she came into Alec's room, he held his breath.

"Okay, Alec," she told him, "I'm going to let you go. The way you feel about the Black . . . well, I just can't keep you here when you have a chance to see him again. Mr. Volence has assured me that everything will be planned carefully. You will do whatever he asks, won't you?"

"Sure, Mum . . . honestly I will!" Alec shouted, throwing his arms around her.

One week later Alec Ramsay flew across the Atlantic Ocean and North Africa in the great *Flying Clipper*. It had been a thrill to ride in the flying ship, but his thoughts were always on the

prospect of seeing his horse again. Nothing could be more exciting than that!

The first leg of their journey was to the desert town of Haribwan. Mr. Volence's friends there gave the businessman useful information about how to find the kingdom of Abu ben Ishak. In Haribwan, Alec learned about the difficulties they would face in their search for the Black.

"We are on the edge of the fertile lands of this country," their host said solemnly. "To the east lie nothing but the barren wastes of the Great Central Desert. The only way to cross it is by caravan, and it is a very dangerous trip."

"Must we cross it?" Mr. Volence asked.

"Yes—if you plan to reach the kingdom of Abu ben Ishak," their host answered. "He lives in the mountains east of the desert. His kingdom is one of the oldest and largest in the land."

"Then we'll go," Mr. Volence said. "What are the dangers you mentioned?"

"Desert raiders," their host replied.

Alec said, "Maybe we won't run into any of them."

"I hope not, but they are the

greatest danger you face. However, travelling with the large caravan I have found for you, you should be safe. Now I want you to meet a young friend of mine who will go along with you."

They went out to the court-yard, and a figure in native clothes walked over to greet them. He was a Bedouin youth, a few years older than Alec, tall and big-boned. His brown, almost liquid eyes peered curiously at them.

"This is Raj," their host said.

"He is on his way to rejoin his tribe. I thought it would be wise for him to accompany you. He has been to the university and can act as your interpreter."

"How do you do," Raj said in English, each word carefully pronounced.

"It's all decided then," Mr. Volence said. "When do we leave?"

"Tomorrow," their host answered. "The caravan leaves Haribwan at day-break."

In the coolness of early morning the caravan moved slowly across the desert, its camels carrying heavy packs securely strapped on to their backs. Raj explained to Alec that their own small unit was part of the great caravan, and they would leave it within a few days' time to head toward the mountains to the east.

"Is that where Abu ben Ishak lives?" Alec asked.

"Yes. Few have seen his home but many know his name. It is there, too, my brother lives."

"How will you find him?"

"It is he who will find me," Raj answered. "He will know of my coming, for word spreads quickly across the desert."

Alec asked no more questions just yet. He was having trouble riding his camel, whose padded feet moved over the hot sand at an awkward pace. His saddle was nothing but a heavy piece of cloth covering the single hump, and there were no stirrups. Alec gripped the sides of the camel tightly with his knees and hung on, hoping it would get easier as the day passed. He was grateful for the native clothes he had been given to wear. The white shawl on his head protected

him from the sun, and the loose outer robe was comfortable in the ever increasing heat.

Day after day the caravan moved through the desert, with the hot sun beating down unmercifully. Slowly Alec got used to the strange gait of his camel, so that his body swayed rhythmically back and forth as he rode. He was becoming so tanned that it wouldn't be long, he decided, before he would be taken for a native! And like the Bedouins he looked forward each night to the luxury of a desert oasis, where they would find fresh water and food and shelter in their tents.

One night Alec couldn't sleep. More than a week had

22

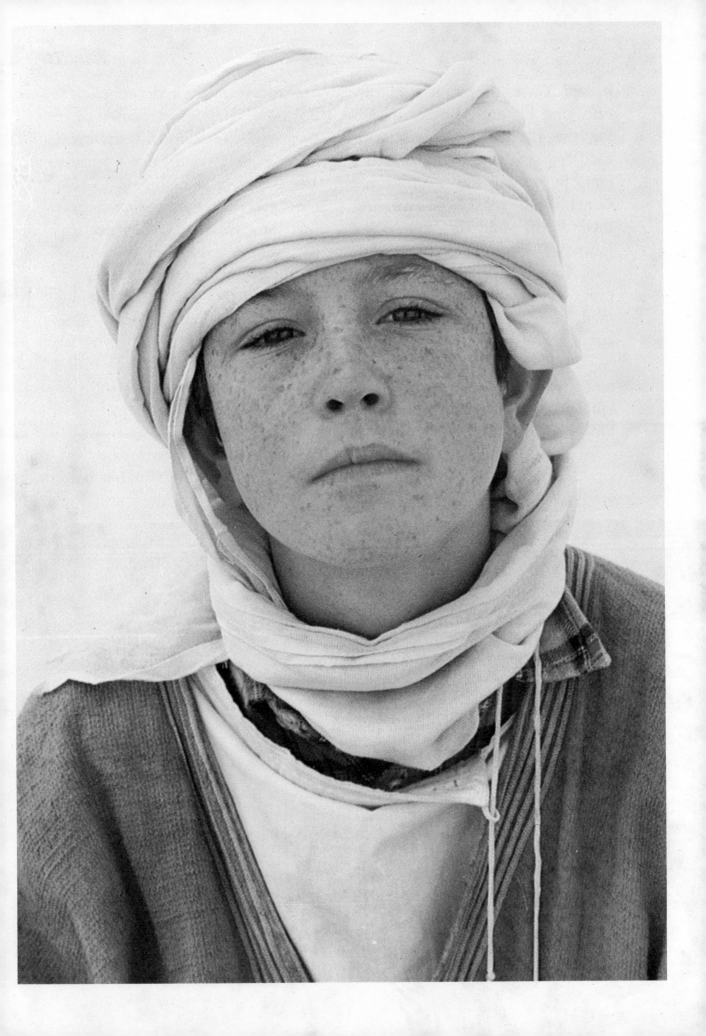

passed since they'd left Haribwan, and his anticipation of seeing the Black had grown with each passing day. Leaving the tent, he found Raj tending his camel, who had been limping toward the end of the day's journey.

"Raj," he said, "have you ever seen this?" Alec held the medallion in his outstretched hand.

Raj's dark eyes narrowed as he took the medallion from Alec. Finally he said, "It is the Phoenix, bird of Arabia, rising again."

"What does it mean?"

"The men who wear it are outcasts from their desert clans," Raj said. "They have formed their own tribe, and like the mythical Phoenix they would rise from the ashes of their banishment to rule the desert for themselves. To do this they would have to destroy the great kingdoms of their most powerful enemies."

"And this would include the kingdom of Abu ben Ishak?" Alec asked.

"Yes, and my brother's kingdom as well," Raj answered. "Tell me, Alec, where did you get this medallion?"

Alec told Raj how he had found the medallion in his barn

the night the Black had been attacked. When he finished, Raj's dark eyes turned to the desert.

"Then it was they who sought to do away with Shêtân," he said. "They will stop at nothing to win the great race of the desert."

"Why?" Alec asked.

"Every five years there is a great race for all tribes," Raj said. "The owner of the winning horse receives his choice of all horses in the race. Such high stakes mean the greatest power, for to lose horses means to weaken a tribe."

"So that's why those desert outlaws wanted to do away with the Black . . . I mean Shêtân," Alec said. "With him out of the race they'd have a chance to win it themselves and become stronger still. Is that right?"

"Yes, a better chance," Raj said. "But my horse, Sagr, is safe, that I know. And with Sagr in the race they could not win—even without Shêtân."

"Your horse will be in the race?"

"Yes, and that is why I am returning," Raj answered.

"When will the race be?"

"Soon now. It is fortunate that tomorrow we will leave the caravan and head for the mountains."

Later, after Raj had left, Alec stayed outside his tent, thinking of all he had learned and wondering if he'd actually see the great race. If so, who from Abu ben Ishak's tribe would be riding the Black? Would the renegades try again to harm the stallion? Were they, even now, planning to do whatever was necessary to keep the Black out of the race?

Alec look around him. The oasis was quiet, hushed, peaceful. Yet Alec was fearful. He felt somehow that danger lay ahead.

At dawn Alec's fears were realized. He was awakened by the cries of the Bedouins and the sound of gunfire. Suddenly Raj appeared at his side and pulled him to his feet.

"Follow me or we'll be killed!" he told Alec.

Together they ran from the back of the tent as turmoil and chaos spread through the camp. Bullets whizzed by their heads as they ran through the shadows to the far side of the oasis. There they jumped into a gully and lay still.

"Keep your head down or it will be blown off!" Raj warned Alec.

"But we've got to help the others!" Alec protested. "There's Mr. Volence, my friend . . ." He stood up and started to turn back, but Raj grabbed him and held him down. A bullet whizzed close by, and Alec flattened himself against the sand.

"We can do nothing now," Raj said.

Alec listened to the fierce, shrill screams of the raiders and knew Raj was right. There was nothing he could do, nothing at all but wait and hope that his friend survived.

"They are the renegades of the medallion," Raj whispered, "and they seek to kill only us, not the others."

"Why *us*?"

"They know it is I who will ride Sagr in the great race," said Raj. "And they have heard of you, Alec, and your power over the mighty black horse Shêtân. They fear you will ride him in the race—and win."

There was another burst of gunfire, and Alec flinched. "Their attack will be over soon," said Raj. "When they do not find us, they will go. Such men are afraid to fight for long—they strike and run."

Alec learned that Raj was right, for soon the gunfire ended and the oasis was quiet except for the bellowing of the camels. Running back to the tents, Alec found Mr. Volence lying on the ground. He was being tended by Bedouins from the caravan.

"I fell running through the brush," his friend explained. "But thank God you're all right. I was so afraid . . ."

"Forget about me," Alec said with concern. "What about you?"

"I think my leg is badly sprained, if not broken," Mr. Volence answered. "It means we must go on with the caravan. I'm sorry, Alec, but I don't think we can make our trip to seek out Abu ben Ishak."

Alec looked at Raj, his face troubled, before turning back to Mr. Volence. "But we've come so far. We're almost there."

"It is only three days more to

the mountains," said Raj.

"I could not make it," Mr. Volence said.

"But *I* can," said Alec. "I can ask Abu ben Ishak to sell you some mares for your farm. He owes me something. He said so when he took the Black from me.

Besides, he *can't* refuse to accept me as his guest. Isn't that right, Raj?"

The Bedouin youth nodded in agreement. "Abu ben Ishak is a man of honour," he said. "If he has offered his help to you, he will give it, and his hospitality also. Our people will never refuse a guest. To do so is considered a sin against Allah."

"Please let me go, Mr. Volence," pleaded Alec.

Troubled and thinking only of Alec's safety, Mr. Volence asked, "Raj, will you accept Alec as your guest and see that he reaches Abu ben Ishak's kingdom without harm?"

"I will," Raj promised. "As Allah is my guide, I will."

"All right, Alec," Mr. Volence said quietly. "I'll wait for you in Haribwan."

The next day Alec, Raj, and a small group of Bedouins set off on their own. Free of the large caravan, they moved at a faster pace than before. But Alec noticed that their guide stopped often, examining fresh tracks in the sand and then changing course.

When Alec asked Raj about it, the young Bedouin told him, "I suspect he senses danger from the renegades."

"Aren't you worried?"

"There is always danger in the desert," Raj answered. "But Allah will protect us."

"I hope so," Alec said. He cast a worried glance at the southern sky, which had suddenly become very dark. There weren't only renegades to worry about, he thought. A storm was brewing if he ever saw one.

Late that night Alec was awakened by a strong wind whistling through the flaps of his tent. He pulled on his clothes and went outside. The desert storm was upon them! Blowing sand peppered his face. The camels were on their feet, moving about uneasily and pulling at their tethers. As Alec stood there the wind grew stronger, the sand heavier.

"*Alec!*" Raj called from somewhere nearby.

Alec staggered in the direction of Raj's voice.

He had gone only a short distance when he stumbled and fell. It was Raj who helped him to his feet. Before them, half-buried in the blowing sand, was the still figure of their guide, his face rigid in death. Stuck in the sand beside him was a sword, and hanging from it was the medallion of the renegades.

The renegades had struck again! Alec recoiled before the silver hilt of the sword. Had it been meant for them? The boy shuddered in spite of himself.

"He has been dead for hours," Raj said. "We can do nothing for him. We must seek cover from the storm."

Clinging together, they made their way back toward camp. They had gone only a short distance when they came upon a camel lying down in the sand.

"Get behind him!" Raj shouted. "Cover your head with your shawl."

They lay there while the wind whistled above their heads and sand covered their bodies. The weight of the sand became heavier and heavier, shutting out the sound of the wind above.

The first indication that the storm was over came hours later when the camel moved his great body. Alec and Raj climbed to their feet, the sand pouring from them.

Only a few stars shone in the sky, for dawn was not far off. There was no sign of the Bedouins or their camels.

"They have gone," Raj said slowly. "They deserted us, fearing

the same fate as that which befell our guide."

Alec stared at Raj in shock. But he knew that what his friend had said was true. They had been left alone, without food or water. To die. . . .

For the next two days they travelled to the east, walking many kilometres on scorching sand under hot, cloudless skies. The constant blistering sun and glare burned Alec's skin black. His eyes were barely slits, and he had trouble seeing. On the afternoon of the second day he fell to his knees, exhausted. Raj helped him to his feet.

"Place your arms around my

31

shoulders, Alec," the young Bedouin said. "You must go on." But
Raj's own eyes were glazed, and
his tongue was swollen from the
heat and lack of water. "Tomorrow . . . tomorrow we will see the
mountains . . . tomorrow, I prom-
ise you."

Another night passed and
Alec awoke to look towards the
east, hoping to see the mountains
Raj had promised. Instead he saw
nothing but a cloud of sand moving rapidly towards them. Was it
another storm? He struggled to a

sitting position, watching the ever
approaching sand cloud.

"Raj," he managed to say.
"Look!" As his friend awoke,
Alec pointed a trembling hand to
the east.

A large group of horsemen
was riding towards them, and the
sound of their mounts' pounding
hoofs shook the desert.

Even though Alec's eyes
were almost swollen shut, he
knew he had never seen a more
magnificent group of horses.
There were blacks, greys and

bays, all galloping swiftly with their heads held high and their coats shining in the rising sun. In the lead was a beautiful chestnut stallion, much larger than any of the others, with a flowing golden mane and tail.

A cry came from Raj's lips as he broke away from Alec and ran towards the chestnut horse and its rider.

The white-robed chieftain on the chestnut's back reached down to grasp Raj's hand. Then they were in each other's arms.

When Alec reached them, Raj said, "This is my brother and . . ." His eyes went to the stallion. "My horse, Sagr, king of all horses in the desert! My brother says he has heard of how we were left to die," Raj continued, "and he promises vengeance on those who committed this crime. But now we must ride with him quickly. The great race is almost at hand."

"But how will I find Abu ben Ishak?" Alec asked. "Will your brother take me to him?"

"He will take you close by, but you must enter Abu ben Ishak's kingdom alone, for we are not welcome there."

"That's fine with me," Alec said. "All I want to do is get there."

Two days later, high in the mountains east of the desert, the Bedouin horsemen came to a halt at a high-peaked pass.

"This is as far as my people will take you," Raj told Alec. "You must go the rest of the way alone on foot. It is not far to Abu ben Ishak's kingdom."

Alec found it hard to say goodbye to his friend. Without Raj, he knew, he never would have made it across the desert.

"I hope we'll see each other again," he said.

"I hope so also, Alec. May Allah guide you and be with you."

When Alec emerged from the pass, he stopped in awe, for the beauty of the valley spread before him was overwhelming. It was deep, rolling tableland, going back to the high cliffs in the distance in the shape of a giant horseshoe.

There was movement on the far side of the valley, and Alec saw a large herd of horses grazing in the shadows. Standing apart from the herd was a giant black horse—*his horse!* Alec whistled and ran down the trail.

The Black whirled, his nose high in the wind, his ears pricked to the sound of Alec's whistle.

Then he screamed a shrill answer, loud and clear. An instant later he ran toward the boy, who was waiting for him.

"Oh, Black . . ." Alec threw his arms around the stallion's neck and held him tight as if he would never let him go again. "It's good, so good to see you again."

A moment later Alec heard the sound of hoofs coming toward them. A white mare, small but beautifully proportioned, was approaching. Her neck was long and graceful like the Black's, and she had the same small head.

Now Alec's gaze turned to the enormous stone residence at the far end of the valley. It rose

storey after storey against the base of the mountains. Alec knew it must be the home of Abu ben Ishak. There was only one way he was going to get there.

He took two short steps forward and swung his legs up while pulling on the Black's mane. Once astride, he gave the stallion his head, and they ran past the tents of startled tribespeople and on to the great stone home.

Abu ben Ishak and a girl dressed in white were waiting outside when Alec brought the Black to a stop in front of them.

There was no surprise in the chieftain's eyes or voice when he said, "Welcome, my young friend. My daughter, Tabari, and I have been waiting for you."

"You mean you were expecting me?"

"Of course. It is my business to know everything that goes on in the desert. It is by the grace of Allah that you arrived in time."

"In time for what?" Alec asked.

"For the race," Abu Ben Ishak answered. "I realize now that no one can ride Shêtân as you do. You are one with him. Will you ride him for my tribe in the great race?"

"Will I? Of course I will, Mr Abu ben Ishak!"

That evening, as Alec sat and ate with Abu ben Ishak and Tabari, the sheikh spoke of how important the coming race was to him and his people.

"Our family has been breeding fine horses for centuries, and Shêtân is the finest of all," Abu ben Ishak said. "We cannot lose him, for he will be bred to our best mares, including Jôhar."

Alec thought of the beautiful white horse he had seen that afternoon. "The white mare?" he asked.

Tabari smiled. "She is mine."

"It will not be easy for you," the sheikh went on, "for this race is like no other. It goes for kilometres across the sand and through the mountains. It tests the speed and endurance of our horses, as it also tests their courage and their hearts. And there are no rules once the race is under way. Our rivals will do anything to stop you."

"They won't be able to catch us," Alec said.

"I hope not," the sheikh answered.

Alec woke early on the day of the race. He dressed and looked out of his bedroom window, wondering what the next few hours would bring to him and the tribe of Abu ben Ishak. Shortly afterwards the old sheikh, riding his grey stallion, led Alec and his people out of the valley to the Plain of Andulla.

Long lines of colourful caravans like their own moved across the plain where the land merged with the white sands of the desert. Clouds of dust rose beneath the hoofs of dancing

horses. The cries and chants of the Bedouins filled the air, and Alec heard his horse's name, "Shêtân, Shêtân," repeated again and again.

A stranger among these people, Alec felt closer to the Black than ever before. He stroked the sleek neck of the stallion. What, he wondered, would be the outcome of this race, which was so important to so many?

When they arrived at the starting point for the race, Abu ben Ishak gave Alec his instructions. "Remember, my young friend, the men who ride against you know the terrain well. It is better that you follow them and do not set the pace. You have studied the map of the course?"

Alec nodded. "I know it," he said.

The beating of drums rose to a new high pitch as Alec lined the

Black up with the other horses. Then he turned to watch the small, wrinkle-faced old man who would start the race. A moment

went by, then another. Suddenly the old man's raised hand swept down. The race was on!

The long line of horses shot forward as one, and Alec heard the frenzied shouts of the Bedouin riders. Then he heard nothing but the pounding of hoofs, felt nothing but the surge of the Black's muscles, saw nothing but the ground slipping away in long, rolling waves beneath him.

Sagr, with Raj riding low on his back, took the lead, and Alec sent the Black after him. He would cling to Sagr's heels across the brush-covered flat and into the mountains. Then, later, as they emerged into the desert he would call upon the Black for his

greatest speed, and he was certain the stallion would not fail him.

But suddenly a grey horse was driven hard against the Black, upsetting Alec's strategy. The rider swung his whip at Alec and locked his leg around the boy's, attempting to push him out of the saddle.

Struggling to regain his balance, Alec pulled himself upright and caught sight of the renegade medallion around the hostile rider's neck! The Black came to a full stop, and Alec remembered Abu ben Ishak's warning—there were no rules in this race. With new determination Alec sent the Black after the trailing horses. He wouldn't be stopped again!

The Black's feet scarcely touched the ground as he passed one horse after another. It wasn't until they left the plain behind and entered a long ravine that Alec drew back on the reins. He

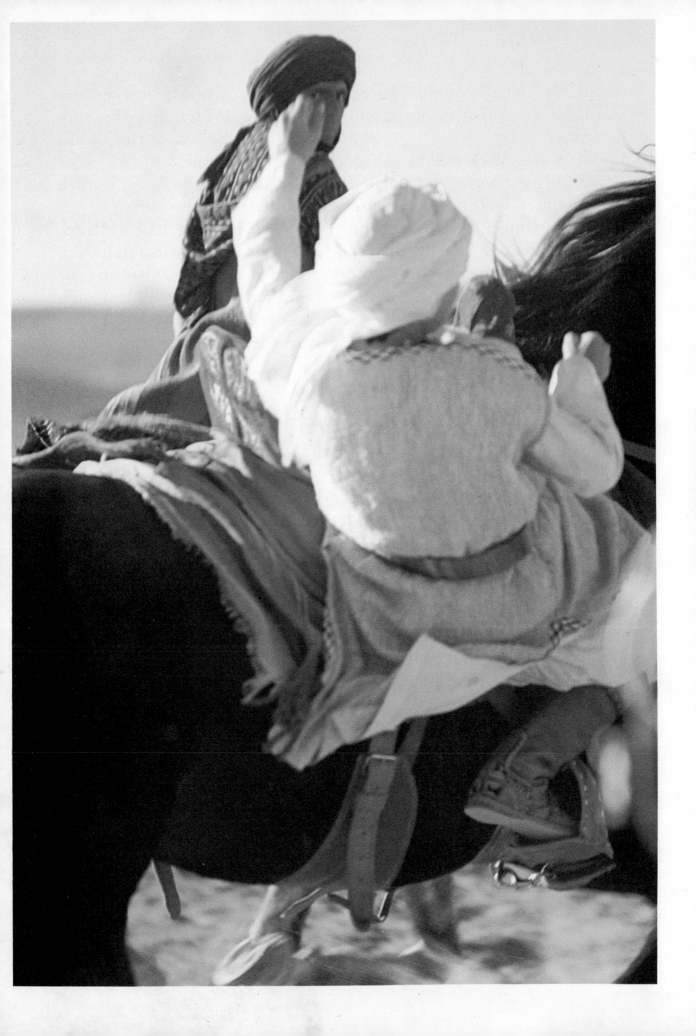

couldn't see Sagr, but just ahead of them was the grey horse and its rider.

As the Black pulled alongside the grey horse, the startled renegade raised his whip again. But this time it was Alec who attacked first. He sent the Black's great body against the other horse, forcing its rider out of his saddle and to the ground!

Alex rode on, knowing that never again would he be in a race such as this. Where was Sagr? Would they ever catch him up?

The course led up a mountainous trail lined with overhanging brush. The branches tore at Alec and the Black, yet Alec felt the stallion gather himself in a great effort to increase his speed. Up and up they went until they reached a great precipice that jutted out over the land below. For a moment Alec thought that they had come to the end of the trail and would be cast into mid air if they went any farther. But the trail wound its way around the end of the precipice and folded once more into the wall of the mountain.

Sagr was nowhere to be seen.

Alec rode on. The beating of the stallion's hoofs was silenced

by the wind, which shrieked and wailed so loudly that the very rock of the mountain walls seemed to vibrate.

"Careful now," he warned the Black. "Watch yourself."

Suddenly the trail widened, and the Black came to a stop. Alec peered ahead. He neither saw nor heard anything, yet he knew the Black had caught Sagr's scent. He moved the stallion on.

The trail wound down to the plains below, and there Alec saw Sagr, with Raj crouched on his back. The Black's eyes rolled. He whistled and the chestnut stallion answered. Then Sagr was away and running.

"Catch him!" Alec shouted to his horse. "If he gets to the desert first, he wins."

The Black bolted after Sagr, and Alec had trouble keeping his seat as the stallion raced down steep gorges and across ravines at

49

a tremendous speed. He drew closer and closer to the chestnut stallion, his head stretched out, his whistle repeating its constant challenge.

There was a break in Sagr's strides as he approached a wide gully. He jumped, clearing it, but he landed hard and his strides were short and jerky as he recovered.

Approaching the gully, Alec let his horse decide for himself when to take off. The Black sprang into the air effortlessly, folding his hocks under his quarters and stretching out his forelegs for landing. He came down without a break in his powerful stride and set out after Sagr with thunder rolling from his hoofs.

Raj knew his way well, and he guided Sagr across the rocky terrain where the going was smoothest. The Black jumped a deep ditch right on Sagr's heels but lost ground to him when the chestnut stallion swerved abruptly, gaining many lengths.

Suddenly there was the sharp crack of a rifle, and the dirt kicked up in front of Sagr! Then there was another shot, and a bullet whizzed by the Black!

Alec pulled hard on his horse, slackening his speed. The gunfire, he saw, was coming from a lorry moving on the far side of the canyon. Alec's blood ran hot with rage, and for the first time in his life he sought revenge. He let out a wild yell of fury and turned the Black towards the moving lorry.

Raj, too, had turned Sagr and was following the lorry. The vehicle careered wildly across the canyon floor as the two riders approached it. Suddenly it swerved dangerously, its brakes ploughing the ground to avoid a deep gully. Alec knew that whoever was driving had applied the brakes too late. Like a lumbering beast, the lorry somersaulted over the edge and disappeared below.

Raj wheeled Sagr around and was once again heading toward the desert, intent upon winning the race!

Run, Black, run!

Alec sat down to ride as he had never ridden before. Sagr cut across the terrain where the ditches were deepest, sliding down the steep sides at full gallop with little loss of stride. The Black followed but Alec did not push

him, choosing to wait for better ground. As Alec listened to the hard-running hoofs of his horse, he couldn't help but think of what the sheikh had told him. This race was like no other. It was a test not only of speed and endurance but of courage and heart as well.

Finally they reached the desert, and Alec knew there was less than a mile to go. Still, he was content to let Raj keep his lead while he waited for the firmer footing of the grassy plain, where the final challenge of courage and speed would come.

Raj constantly looked behind him, and Alec knew that his friend was worried.

The Black's wind-tangled mane whipped back in Alec's face. "Come on," he told his horse. "Let's get him now!"

The Black swept over the sand, drawing closer and closer to the flying Sagr. As they neared the Plain of Andulla, Raj glanced back and saw the Black at his mount's hindquarters. There was no friendliness in the young Bedouin's dark eyes now, only grim determination that Sagr would not be passed!

Alec knew he had to be careful in pulling his horse away from Sagr. A mistake at this speed meant certain death. His wind-blurred eyes made it difficult to gauge distances.

There was a horrible impact of running bodies before Alec was successful in getting the Black clear of Sagr. Then both horses were off in a dead run to the finish. Stride for magnificent stride, they moved together. Stirrup to stirrup, Alec and Raj raced across the plain, their bodies, like their horses', straining, sweating, and powdered with dust.

As he entered the path to the finishing line, Alec saw Raj glance at him; his friend realised that he was beaten. Slowly the Black inched ahead of Sagr until he was in front by a head, then a neck, as they swept towards the finishing line.

The roar of the crowd was deafening. Hearing it, Alec was moved as he had been only once before in his life—at the end of the match race against Cyclone and Sun Raider. Then, as now, the Black had proved his greatness. But this time he had proved it against the worst possible odds—not on a racetrack, but across perilous mountain trails and miles of desert wilderness.

"Oh, Black," he shouted as they swept across the finishing line. "We did it! We did it!"

A few moments later the desert air was tense and quiet. Abu ben Ishak, owner of Shêtân, strode slowly among the horses that had been in the race, making his selection of those he would take with him. When he reached Sagr, he looked not at the chestnut stallion but at Alec, who stood beside Raj.

"Well, Alec? You look troubled for one who has won such a race."

Alec met the chieftain's gaze. "Raj is my friend. I'd hate to see him lose his horse."

"Because he is your friend his horse will be spared," Abu ben Ishak said, and he walked on.

Raj's hand grasped Alec's. "May Allah always be with you, my friend."

The following day Abu ben Ishak led his tribespeople and his new herd of horses home. Later, as he and Alec watched them grazing in his lush pastures, the sheikh said, "I need not tell you that I am very grateful. That you know. I know too of your great love for Shêtân and his for you." He paused. "Shêtân means very much to me, but I would like to give him to you." Abu ben Ishak handed Alec the Black's halter and waved him towards the tall stallion.

Alec walked to his horse, put his arms around the small head, and held him close.

Finally he said, "I can't take him, sir. He belongs here with you and all your mares. You've got to finish what you started—breeding the best horses in the world." His gaze turned to the beautiful white mare standing nearby. "There's Jôhar," he added. "She's the best of them all. What a foal she will have!"

"And that foal shall be yours, my friend," Abu ben Ishak said.

"Mine?" Alec asked incredulously.

The Black would always be a part of him, Alec knew, but the great stallion belonged here. Now Alec would let himself think only of Jôhar's foal to come. Perhaps it would be a colt, a son of the Black! It would be his alone to rear and train, maybe even to race, as he had the Black! His eyes shining, Alec turned to Abu ben Ishak, and together they walked towards the house.

The Black Stallion returns to his birthplace
—and Alec Ramsay follows him! Across the
burning Arabian sands...to a hidden valley
where the swiftest horses in the world are bred...
to a thrilling—and dangerous—race that will
decide the fate of an entire desert kingdom!

SCHOLASTIC INC.

0-590-72227-1